THIS BOOK BELONGS TO:

....

WITH LOVE FROM:

....

PARIS FASHION WEEK

PARIS FASHION WEEK

PARIS FASHION WEEK

The Claris Collection:
The Chicest Mouse in Paris
Fashion Show Fiasco

*For my daughter, Gwyn –
may your future be filled with big
adventures through Paris!*

Hardie Grant
EGMONT

Claris: Fashion Show Fiasco
published in 2019 by
Hardie Grant Egmont
Ground Floor, Building 1, 658 Church Street
Richmond, Victoria 3121, Australia
www.hardiegrantegmont.com

Designed by Pooja Desai

A catalogue record for this
book is available from the
National Library of Australia

ISBN: 9781760502874

Printed in China by Asia Pacific Offset

1 3 5 7 9 10 8 6 4 2

Claris

THE CHICEST MOUSE IN PARIS

Fashion
Show
Fiasco

Megan Hess

Springtime was blooming in beautiful Paris,

and life was *très belle* for sweet little Claris.

She'd just moved in to her own tiny flat,
with two lovely parents – and their daughter, the brat.

Designing new dresses was Claris's passion,
with help from Monsieur, who knew all about fashion.

One morning, the friends nibbled fruit from a tray,
and they heard Madame say, 'Well, today is the day!
It's better than birthdays, and certainly Christmas.
There's no way, *mes chéris*, that we'd ever miss this!'

Claris waited for Madame to further explain,
but the brat interrupted. She was such a pain!

She whinged and she whined and she kicked up a stink.
'I'm not leaving this house till I'VE HAD MY DRINK!'

As the butler raced in with some tea (and a frown) ...

... the table was bumped and some paper fell down.

It landed near Claris, who let out a squeak.
An invite to Chanel at – *mon dieu* – Fashion Week!

No wonder Madame was excited to go.
This mouse only *dreamed* of attending that show!

As Madame placated her terrible daughter,
and showed all the dresses she'd already bought her,

Monsieur beamed at Claris. 'This week's a big deal!
You should dream up some looks with dramatic reveal.
For when you're in Paris and it's Fashion Week,
you might see a show – and you cannot look meek.'

FASHION WEEK
OUTFITS

☐ DIOR
☐ CHANEL
☐ GIVENCHY
☐ SAINT LAURENT
☐ CHLOÉ
☐ CELINE

So Claris raced back to her atelier,
and made all-new outfits with absolute flair!

A tweed look for Chanel, a fun frock for Dior,
a Givenchy-style dress, all with drama galore.

As Claris was stitching her final design
(a Valentino style with a crazy neckline),

the family was leaving, Madame all aglow,
and all three in couture from their heads to their toes.

'But oh no!' Claris cried, and her heart gave a tug.
Madame's invitation was still on the rug!

Without it, she would be declined at the door.
She'd miss out on Chanel, and perhaps even more.

But what could she do? So small was our Claris.
The Chanel show was far – in fact, right across Paris.
As she puzzled and pondered, someone rang the bell.
A man bringing flowers. Our mouse knew him well!

She looked at Monsieur and then hatched a plan.
'Let's hide in the bike of the delivery man!
With your Fashion Week know-how and all our street smarts,
we'll get to Madame right before the show starts.'

Monsieur and Claris climbed among the bouquets,
and before they could blink they were off on their way.

The bike zoomed along down the wide avenues,
past beautiful buildings in elegant hues.

Their ride stopped outside an incredible store.
'Givenchy,' sighed Claris, and gazed up in awe.

In front was a dog in a classic bow tie,
and Monsieur cried, 'Hubert! Let's go and say hi.'

'*Bonjour*, my old friend,' Monsieur said. 'What a day!
We must get to Chanel – do you know the way?'

Hubert smiled back. *'J'adore* this time of year!
That scooter just there will get you quite near.'

'*Merci!*' Claris waved, and off they careened.
She was *the* chicest mouse that the bulldog had seen.

They twisted and turned through Tuileries park,
past the Arc de Triomphe – an iconic landmark.

But as they swung round a corner, Monsieur lost his grip!
Would this be the end of their last-minute trip?

Claris threw him her belt and said, 'HOLD ON TIGHT!'
Then she pulled him to safety with all of her might.

Monsieur said, 'You saved me! I'd almost let go!
Claris, you're the bravest little mouse that I know.'

'That's what friends are for!' and she straightened her gown.
'Now surely we're close, we've been all over town!'

As they jumped off the scooter in front of Dior,
both cat and mouse gasped at the person they saw.

The Maestro of Fashion in a long velvet bow,
a Chanel invite in hand, on her way to the show.

Monsieur looked at Claris and said, 'Are you ready?
Let's hide in her handbag, the great Hermès Kelly!'

And with that plan in mind, like Bonnie and Clyde,
they leapt into her bag – their next place to hide.

The Maestro walked in to the famed Chanel show,
never knowing that she had two small friends in tow.

There was glitz, there was glam, people dressed with such passion.
It was weird, it was wild, but *darrrrling*, that's fashion!

Claris longed to explore, but she still had her quest.
'*How* will we find them among all these guests?'

Monsieur raised a brow. 'If I know that brat
we'll soon hear her screaming – I *am* sure of that.'

And then right on cue, like an actor on stage,
the daughter yelled out in a terrible rage.

'There they are!' Claris cried. 'So let us stay focused
and deliver the invite without being noticed.'

They leapt onto a lamp post
with absolute skill.
Monsieur dangled her down
with nothing but twill.

As Claris got closer,
her heart skipped a beat,
but she slipped in the invite,
so very discreet.

CHANEL
Invitation
PARIS FASHION WEEK

They'd made it in time!
The show was beginning.
As the family gained entry,
Madame, she was grinning.

CHANEL
Invitation
PARIS FASHION WEEK

CHANEL

CHANEL

Claris was thrilled – they had just saved the day!
'But aren't you sad?' Monsieur said. 'Things did not go your way.
It would have been lovely to see Chanel's show.'

'My chic feline friend,' she replied, 'oh, no no!

'We raced through the city with flowers and Dior,
hitched a ride with Hermès, met a bulldog and more!

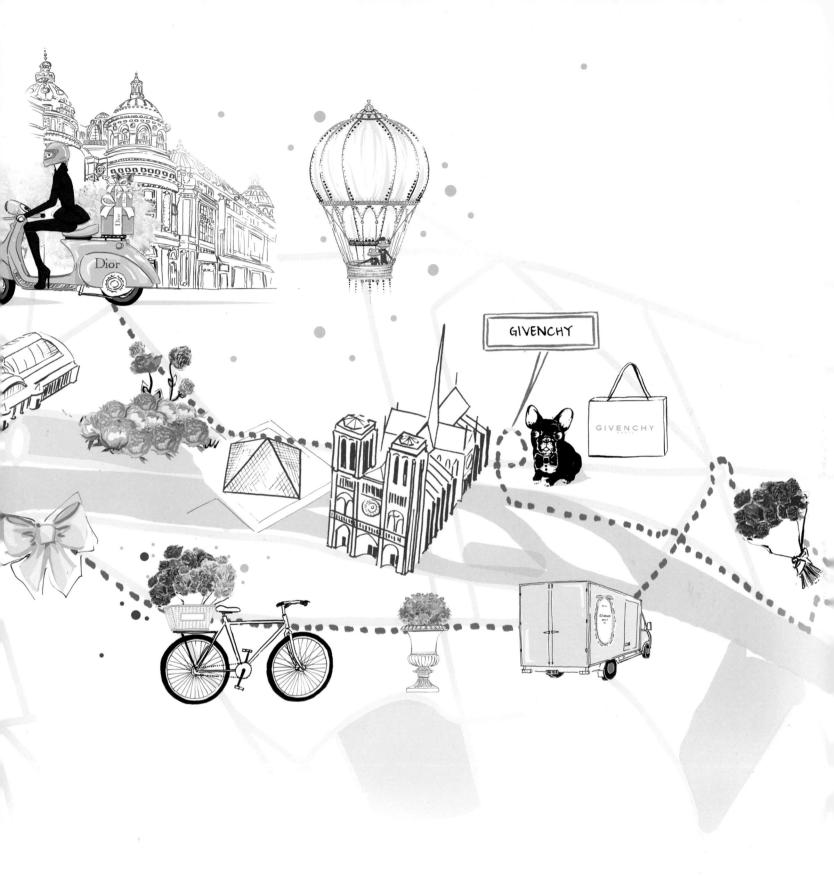

And all with my friend, whom I truly adore.
Having you, Monsieur dear, I now need nothing more.'

He beamed and then said, 'Well, my kind-hearted mouse,
I have a surprise – the best seats in the house!'

Claris had dreamed of a real fashion show,
but never believed she'd one day get to go.

And yet there was Claris, overcome with delight,
the best-dressed of Paris seated all to her right.

They were high on a beam, watching closely below.
They were *the* fashion stars of the chic Chanel show.

Megan Hess is an acclaimed fashion illustrator who works with some of the most prestigious designers and luxury brands around the world, such as Chanel, Dior, Cartier, Prada, Fendi, Louis Vuitton and Tiffany & Co.

Fashion Show Fiasco is the second book in her beloved *Claris* collection.

Visit Claris at claristhemouse.com
and follow her adventures on Instagram @claristhemouse